THE SEA KING

IN RUSSIAN FOLKLORE, THE MORSKOI
TSAR WAS THE KING OF THE SEA.
HIS DAUGHTERS WERE BEAUTIFUL
MAIDENS KNOWN AS RUSULKAS WHO
APPEARED ON THE WATER AS SWANS,
GEESE, DUCKS, OR SPOONBILLS.
THE SEA KING LIVED UNDER THE WATER IN
CRYSTAL HALLS OF GREAT GRANDEUR.
HE LEFT HIS PALACE ONLY TO SEARCH OUT
A HUMAN VICTIM. HAVING DAUGHTERS
OF HIS OWN, HE ESPECIALLY SOUGHT BOYS
OR PRINCES — WHO INEVITABLY CARRIED
OFF OR MARRIED ONE OF THE DAUGHTERS.

Published simultaneously in 2003 in Great Britain and Canada by

TRADEWIND BOOKS LIMITED
www.tradewindbooks.com

Distribution and Representation in the UK by Turnaround   www.turnaround-uk.com

Text copyright © 2003 by Jane Yolen and Shulamith Oppenheim
Illustrations copyright © 2003 by Stefan Czernecki

Book design and title type by Elisa Gutiérrez
Assistant to illustrator: Elisa Gutiérrez

The typeface used in the book is Insignia.

10 9 8 7 6 5 4 3 2 1

Cataloguing-in-Publication Data for this book is available from The British Library.

National Library of Canada Cataloguing in Publication Data

Yolen, Jane.
   The sea king

ISBN 1-896580-46-7

1. Mermen—Juvenile literature. I. Oppenheim, Shulamith Levey. II. Czernecki, Stefan, 1946- II. Title.
GR910.Y64 2002   j398.21   C2002-910246-4

Printed and bound in Korea

The publisher thanks the Canada Council for the Arts and the British Columbia Arts Council for their support.

Canada Council   Conseil des Arts
for the Arts   du Canada

BRITISH
COLUMBIA
ARTS COUNCIL

THE SEA KING

JANE YOLEN & SHULAMITH OPPENHEIM

ILLUSTRATED BY STEFAN CZERNECKI

VANCOUVER · TRADEWIND BOOKS · LONDON

Once in a certain land,
in a certain kingdom, there
was a king who was out shooting.
He aimed at an eagle.

"Do not shoot me," cried the eagle.
"Some day I shall be useful to you."

So the king relented, and took the
eagle back to his palace.

There the eagle ate and ate and
ate some more until there was
nothing left in the kingdom — no
cattle, grain, fruits, or fish.

"How is this useful to me?"
asked the worried king.

"Climb on my back," said
the eagle, "and you
shall see."

So the king climbed upon the eagle's back and away they flew over the ocean. Then three times the eagle dropped the king into the water and three times plucked him from the waves.

"Now my king, you know the fear of death just as I did," said the eagle, and the king agreed.

They flew on until they came upon a boat, and the eagle set the king down upon it, saying, "Now I will leave you, sire. But on the boat you will find two coffers, one green, one red. Do not open them until you are home. Open the red one in the back garden and the green in the front garden."

And away the eagle flew, leaving the king alone on the boat.

Before long the king came to a certain island. On going ashore, his curiosity overcame him and he opened the red coffer. Out came so many cows, there was hardly room on the little island for them all.

"How shall I gather this herd together?" the king wondered aloud. Then, suddenly he beheld a man rising up out of the water who had a fish tail instead of legs and a crown on his head.

"I shall gather your herd," said the sea man, "and put them back into the red coffer, but only on one condition."

"Name it," said the king.

"I am the Morskoi Tsar, the king of the sea. Give me that which you do not know is in your house."

The king thought: I know everything in my house. And so he agreed.

Then the Morskoi Tsar did as he had promised, and the king sailed happily for home.

What should he learn on returning home? His wife had given birth to a son!

He wept as he held the child, fearing to tell his wife the truth — that all unknowing, he had promised the boy to the sea king.

But then he smiled, thinking: This Morskoi Tsar does not know where I live.

So having convinced himself that his son was safe, the king went out into the back garden and opened the red coffer. Out came cattle and sheep and goats beyond counting.

Then he went into the front garden and opened the green coffer. There appeared flowers and fruits of every size and hue.

The king was in such rapture at the return of all the eagle had eaten — and more — that he promptly forgot the promise he made to the sea king.

Years passed. But promises do not.

One day the king was walking by the river. Suddenly out of the water came the very same sea man who said, "You have forgotten your debt to the Morskoi Tsar. Now you must pay."

What could the king do? He went back and told the queen and the prince the truth. They wept together. But at last the prince said, "Mother, Father, you have always told me to tell the truth. You have always cautioned me to keep my word." So he walked down to the water's edge and waited.

He waited and waited some more. When nothing happened at the water's edge, he tired of waiting and he turned and walked into the woods. Soon he found a little hut that stood on spindly chicken feet. In that hut — though he did not know it — lived Baba Yaga, the witch. When she heard him, she came out of the hut and smiled at him with her iron teeth.

The prince spoke to her politely, as his parents had taught him to behave, which was lucky. Otherwise she might have eaten him.

"Go back to the seashore, my son," she said. "There twelve spoonbills will turn into twelve lovely maidens bathing. Take the dress of the eldest. Then you will be ready to go to the Morskoi Tsar."

"Thank you, grandmother," said the prince, again politely. This was lucky as she still could have eaten him.

So the prince went back to the shore and did as Baba Yaga instructed. Once he had hold of her dress, the eldest maiden could not fly away.

"Please return what you have taken," she said, "and I shall be useful to you."

He did so, but asked, "Pray tell me your name."

"Vasilisa the Wise," she said. Then she put on her dress, turned into a spoonbill, and flew after her sisters toward the setting sun.

Now the prince set off to find the Morskoi Tsar, swimming deeper and deeper into the water, until at last he came to a great palace with walls of shimmering crystal. Swimming in front was the very same sea king that his father had met so long ago.

"I have been waiting for you," said the Morskoi Tsar. "But as your father was slow in sending you to me, you must now build me a crystal bridge in one night, or else you will lose your head."

The prince sat down in front of the sea king's palace and wept because of course he could do no such thing. "Alas, my mother, alas my father," he cried, "I shall see you no more."

Along came Vasilisa, the girl who had been the spoonbill. "Go to sleep. The morning is wiser than the evening."

She sang him to sleep and when he was snoring, gave a mighty whistle. From everywhere swam fish-tailed workmen to do her bidding, and the bridge was completed before sunrise.

Then Vasilisa woke the prince, who was greatly relieved. She handed him a broom and he swept the bridge clean.

"Bravo!" said the Morskoi Tsar. "But there is yet another task. I desire a garden by tomorrow — tall trees flowering with ripe fruit and birds flying everywhere. Otherwise I will have your head."

The prince sat in front of the sea king's palace and wept because of course he could not do any such thing. "Alas, my mother, alas my father," he cried, "I shall see you no more."

Along came Vasilisa once again. "Go to sleep. The morning is wiser than the evening."

She sang him to sleep and when he was snoring, gave a mighty whistle. From everywhere came fish-tailed gardeners to do her bidding, and by morning there was a garden to gladden the heart of any sea king.

When the Morskoi Tsar saw the garden, he smiled.

"You have done well twice," said the Morskoi Tsar. "And I would be glad to have you as my son-in-law. Choose a bride from my twelve daughters. But beware. They all look alike. If you choose the same girl three times, she will be your wife. But if you mistake one for another, I will have your head."

"Do not worry," Vasilisa whispered to the prince. "I will marry you. So listen carefully. The first time I shall wave a handkerchief. The second time I shall adjust my dress. The third time a fly shall settle on my head."

The prince nodded.

Then out came the twelve sisters, dressed alike in red dresses with white embroidery. Their headdresses were exactly the same as well. They were all tall and strong-boned, with eyes the color of the sea.

"Choose," said the Morskoi Tsar.

The prince looked carefully and, as he did, one of the princesses waved a handkerchief. "That one," he said.

The sea king smiled. "Again."

This time the twelve princesses danced around and around and when they finally came to a halt they looked as alike as herrings on a plate. But one of them pulled at the skirt of her dress.

"That one," said the prince.

The Morskoi Tsar smiled. "Again," he said.

This time when the twelve princesses shifted around, the prince was turned around as well. And when they had all stopped, the sea king said, "No one is to move."

All of the princesses stood still. But a little fly flew round and about one of the princesses and landed upon her headdress.

"That one," said the prince, pointing.

The sea king smiled. Vasilisa smiled. And the prince smiled, too.

So the prince and Vasilisa the Wise were married and, after their fathers died, they ruled both land and sea for the rest of their days.